FLEA'S BEST FRIEND

CHARLES FUGE

Gareth Stevens Publishing
MILWAUKEE

For a free color catalog describing Gareth Stevens' list of high-quality books, call 1-800-542-2595 (USA) or 1-800-461-9120 (Canada).
Gareth Stevens' Fax: (414) 225-0377.

Library of Congress Cataloging-in-Publication Data available upon request from publisher. Fax: (414) 225-0377 for the attention of the Publishing Records Department.

ISBN 0-8368-1292-1

North American edition first published in 1995 by
Gareth Stevens Publishing
1555 North RiverCenter Drive, Suite 201
Milwaukee, Wisconsin 53212, USA

Original edition published in 1994 by Pan Macmillan Children's Books.

Printed in the United States of America

2 3 4 5 6 7 8 9 99 98 97 96 95

Flea loved dogs.
He lived on one with his mom and dad (and his brothers and sisters!).
One day, Flea decided to leave.
“I’m going to find my very own home!” he thought.

So off he hopped in search of something better, and first he found . . .

Sausage, the Basset Hound

She had short legs — not much use for scratching — but her back was very l-o-n-g.

It took Flea six good leaps and a couple of somersaults to get from one end to the other.

Exhausted, Flea hopped off in search of something better and found . . .

Frinkle, the Shar-Pei Puppy

She looked soft and baggy.
"Lovely," thought Flea, nestling down among the wrinkles.
Flea sank deeper and deeper into the folds — until he realized he was stuck.
It took him hours to struggle out again.

After a short rest, Flea stretched his legs and hopped off in search of something better and found . . .

Graham, the Great Dane

There was plenty of room
on Graham! Flea leapt onto
a paw and began to climb.
It took days to reach the top.
Flea looked around.
He could see for miles!
Then he looked down.
Flea felt dizzy.
He had no head for heights.

Sliding all the way down
Graham's back, Flea hopped
off in search of something
better and found . . .

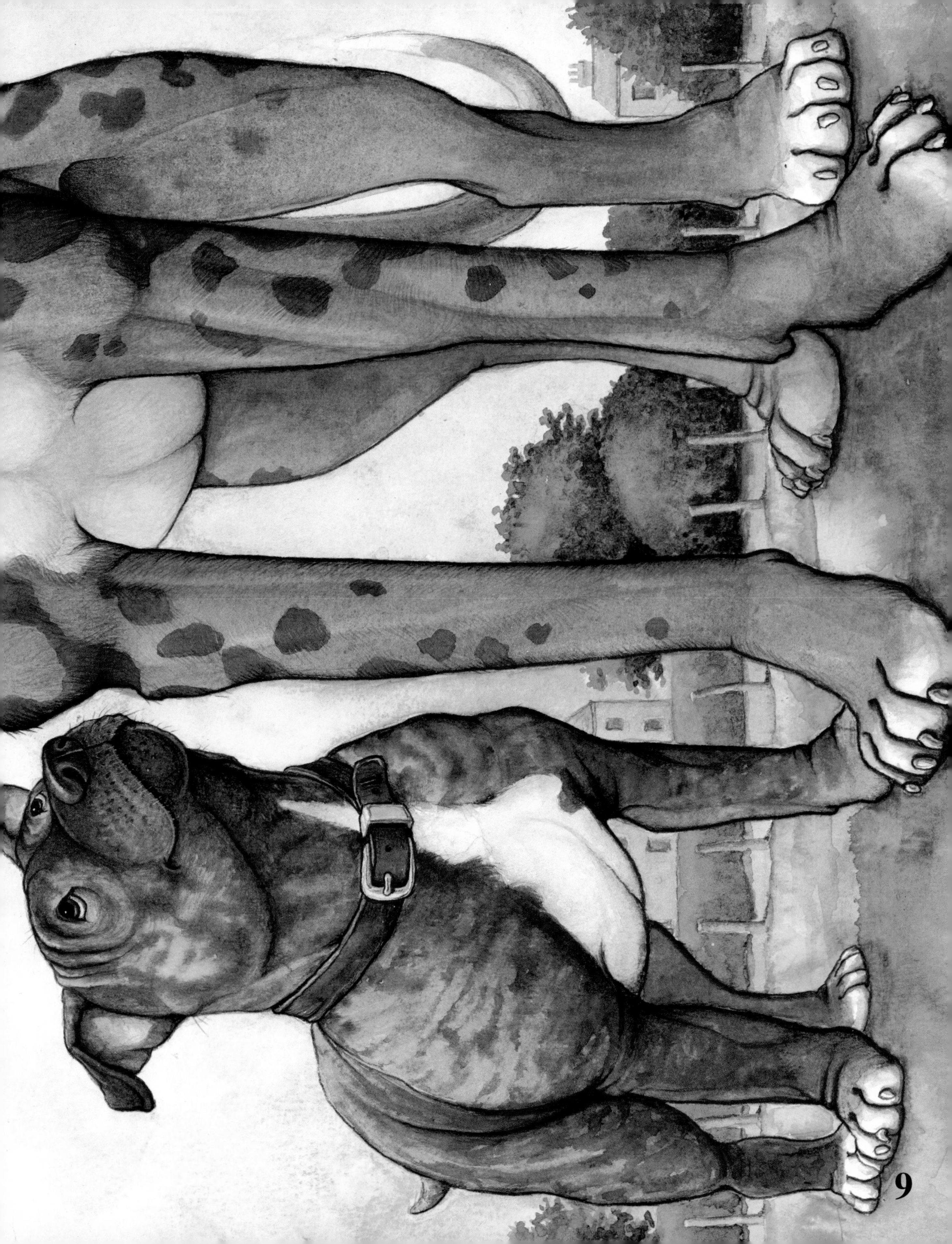

Mike, the Bull Terrier

Mike was short and stocky.
"Looks more secure," thought Flea, jumping onto Mike's pink muzzle.
But where would Flea hide?
There was only one small patch where he couldn't be seen.
"Not much room for an active flea," he thought.

Disappointed, he hopped off in search of something better and found . . .

Iggy, the Greyhound

There would be plenty of exercise with Iggy,
who was itching to start the race.
They were off . . . !
But Flea could scarcely hold on as they sped
around the track.

A little shaky, Flea hopped off in search of
something better and found . . .

Fletch, the Bulldog

He wasn't moving fast.
He wasn't moving at all.
Fletch was fast asleep in his favorite armchair.
"Splendid!" thought Flea, leaping aboard.
He had just settled himself comfortably behind
Fletch's left ear . . . when Fletch began to SNORE . . .
HHUNHK — HHROOAAR — ZZzzz
HHUNHK — HHROOAAR — ZZzzz.

Flea spent two sleepless nights with Fletch,
then he hopped off in search of something better.
He found . . .

Fuzz, the Pekingese

"Peace, at last!" thought Flea, curling up in Fuzz's long, silky coat.
But no sooner had he closed his eyes . . .
POOF!
A cloud of flea powder came puffing at him from above.

Gasping for air, Flea leapt for safety and went in search of something better.
It was some time before he found . . .

Chutney, the Pointer

He was out in the country looking for rabbits. Perched on Chutney's nose, Flea enjoyed the fresh air as the pointer rushed from bush to bush. Then Chutney stopped short.

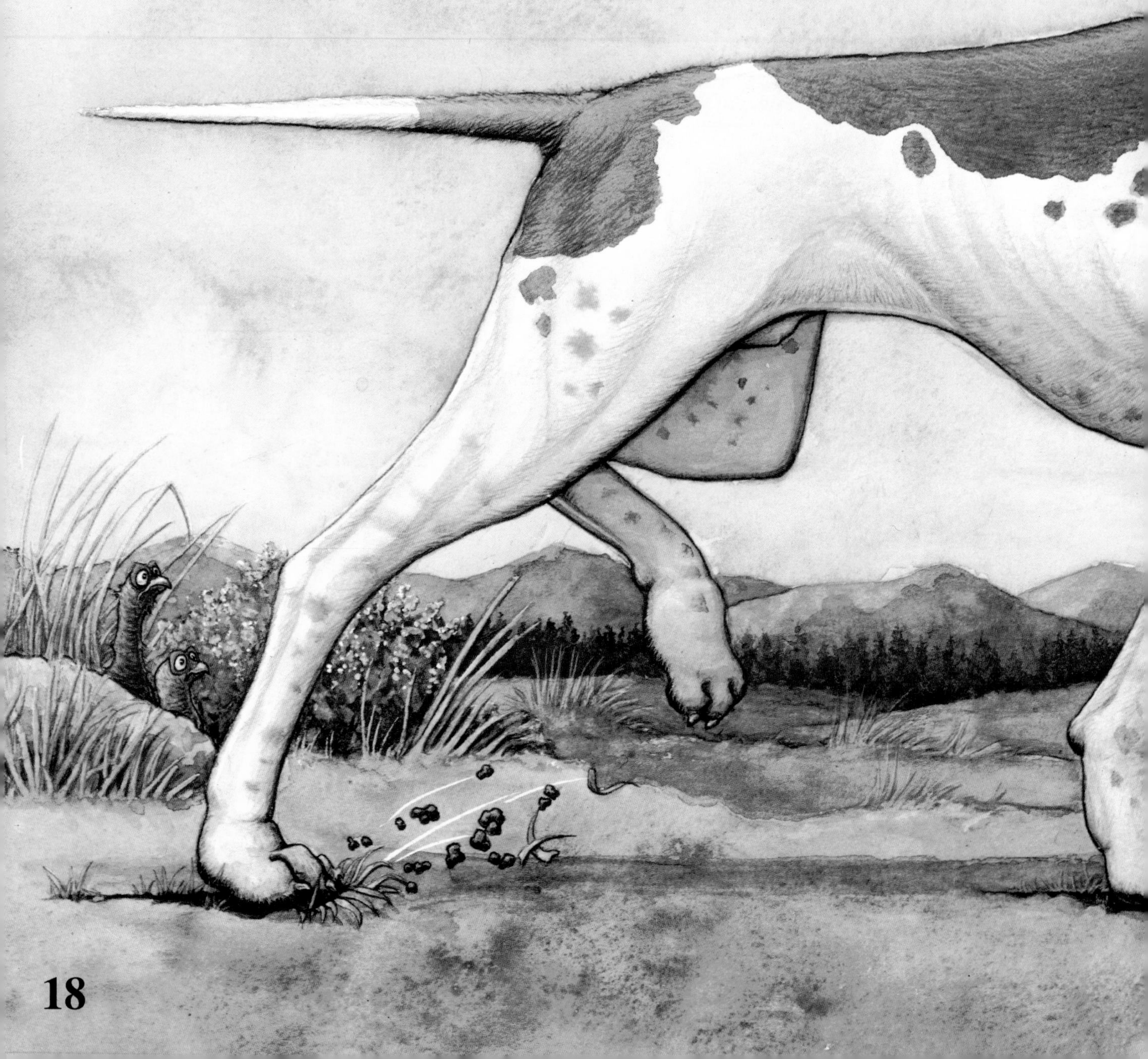

Flea flew off — PLOP!
Straight into the river where he found . . .

Colin, the Retriever

"Help!" sputtered Flea.
He couldn't swim.
Colin retrieved his stick — and
Flea as well, who grabbed Colin's fur
as he climbed out of the water.
Flea was wet.
Colin was wet.
He shook and shook himself dry
until Flea was tossed off his back
in a shower of droplets.

Flea squished miserably back to
the city in search of something better.
There he found . . .

Curly, the Chinese Crested

Except for a tuft on the top of her head and one on the end of her tail, Curly had no hair at all! Poor Flea was getting desperate.
"No harm in trying," he thought, and up he jumped. There was *nothing* to hold on to.

Skidding and sliding, Flea slithered straight off the smooth, slippery skin and found . . .

SOMETHING BETTER — a mongrel and
the scruffiest dog in town.
Flea looked her up and down.
She wasn't too long, and she wasn't too tall.
She didn't move fast or stop too quickly.
She never took a bath and snored
only sometimes.

"Marvelous," said Flea out loud.
"A home at last — and HOME is what I'll call her!"